ZOMBUNNY
craig crawford

GRAVESIDE✶PRESS

For a list of potentially triggering content,
please skip to page 36.

"Daddy, I need him!"

Frank looked up from a rotating display case of amusing buttons. He'd hauled Penny with him to one of his favorite stores, The Dancing Spider, to give Sara a break. The Spider was one of those eclectic shops catering to people looking for unique and non-politically correct gifts, and the place always put a grin on his face.

On the other hand, they specialized in toys...sometimes really *odd* toys. Frank knew with certainty he wasn't getting out without buying Penny something, and he looked down to see what treasure she'd uncovered from the shelves.

Only six, she already showed a quirky side. She had a penchant for creepy things—something Frank blamed on Sara, who thrived on horror books, movies, and even knick-knacks. They'd agreed on keeping Penny away from spooky movies at least until she was ten, but the girl seemed to gravitate toward anything odd and eerie.

Penny stood in a blue dress and her "clacking" shoes, as she liked to call them, holding up her find. Her grin stretched the width of her face. She thrust her hands upward, displaying a bright green stuffed animal.

It took a second look for Frank to realize it was actually a bunny. Half the size of Penny, it sported large, oval black eyes stitched into the face. Its long, black mouth stretched the width of its head, complete with cross stitches like it had been sewn shut. Its intentionally tattered ears displayed the same loud green. A black fabric skull and crossbones tattooed its belly.

"What is that?" Frank asked, fully prepared for the pitch.

Penny's eyes widened. "It's a zombie bunny," she declared. "He's cute and soft and...Daddy, he's wonderful."

The bunny had an oversized forehead, and he tried to understand how she found it adorable. He sighed, running a hand over its head. "It is soft. Really soft. I see why you like it." The price tag made him pause. "He's kind of expensive, hon."

"I don't care. Daddy, you can keep my allowance for however long it takes to buy him. I've got money in my box at home. Please? Daddy, he really needs me."

Frank considered. Penny didn't ask for things much, and he had known what bringing her along meant. "Hmmn..." The hopeful look in her pleading eyes smashed his will. "It's going to cost you a month's allowance."

"I don't care."

He really couldn't see the beauty of the rabbit other than the soft material. "The next time we go out, you won't be able to get other toys."

"That's fine. Zombie Bunny needs to live with me."

He gave in. Penny bounced up and down. The bunny's ears flopped about as she danced in the aisle. Frank grabbed himself a postcard and headed to the counter.

A young woman nodded as Penny set her newfound friend on the counter. "Whoa, that's a big rabbit." Her brow furrowed to form a frown form under her mask. "Where did you find him?"

Penny pointed to the corner.

"I don't remember getting those. Was it the only one?"

Penny nodded vigorously. "He's the last one."

"Huh. Cheryl must have ordered them." She nodded. "My partner is always buying things from oddball distributors. But he's got a price tag, so we're good."

The cashier rang everything up and Frank paid.

"Would you like a bag for your new friend, or are you just going to carry him?"

"I'll carry him, thank you. He's my new best friend."

"What are you going to name him?" the young woman asked.

"Zombunny. He told me he likes that."

"Appropriate. Well, I'm glad we've put a smile on your face today. Thank you for shopping," the woman said.

"I'm glad we could help you out," Frank told her. "You've made my daughter a happy girl."

Penny talked to her stuffed rabbit all the way home. Frank glanced at her in the rearview mirror as she tested the seams and stuffing, squeezing it with all her strength. She sat enraptured in the back seat, and Frank was content with his decision to let her buy it.

Penny popped her seatbelt and got out as soon as the car stopped. She raced to the front door with both arms clamped around the big green creepy rabbit, its ears jouncing as she ran. Frank only snorted and followed her in.

Penny's thirteen-year-old brother Devin eyed Frank as he closed the door. "What's that thing you let her get?"

Frank shook his head. "Some stuffed rabbit she found at

The Spider. I know, it's kind of ugly and creepy, but your sister's in love with it."

Devin rolled his eyes. "How much did it cost?"

"Never you mind."

"Uh-huh. Mom's gonna kick your butt."

"Go do homework or something." Frank headed to the kitchen.

Penny's voice blared loud and clear, but the words poured out so fast she was barely coherent. Frank found her standing in front of her mother, holding Zombunny as she told her the entire story.

"Isn't he so cute, Momma? I'm going to make a place for him next to me on my pillow and take him out to play with the other kids."

Sara eyed Frank but grinned. "A zombie bunny, huh? He's definitely our kind of rabbit."

"Yes he is, Momma! I'm going to show him my room." Penny headed out the doorway. "Thanks Daddy!"

"I couldn't help it," he said. "You saw the look on her face."

"How much was he?"

"Over thirty bucks." Frank shrugged. "I've spent more on less. She said we could take it out of her allowance."

"As happy as she is, we'll split it with her. She doesn't get this excited about toys very often."

"It's what I thought too." He chuckled. "He's almost too big to hold on to with that round head. He's really soft, though. Did you feel the material?"

"It's some kind of ultra-soft fleece," Sara said. "I'd use him for a pillow."

"We'll see how long it takes for her to squeeze the stuffing out of him."

***

The following weekend, Frank overheard Penny talking in her room. He peeked in and found her sitting on the bed, holding her zombie rabbit by its fuzzy hands. "What'cha up to?"

"Just playing. He can make words."

"What?"

On the bunny's big forehead, the word *frend* showed in the soft green fleece. Frank started laughing. "That's not how you spell 'friend,' hon."

"I know," she said, "But there wasn't enough room on his head to spell it right. It's okay. He doesn't know words like me."

"That's pretty cool, actually. Can I see him?"

"Sure, Daddy."

Frank took up the rabbit and slowly rubbed his fingers

along its face. He discovered rubbing in one direction erased Penny's word. Tracing his finger in the soft material, he was able to draw lines in the fabric. "Huh." He handed it back. "It was made with really good material."

"I know. Daddy—you made eyebrows!"

"He looked like he could use eyebrows, but you can erase them if you want."

She smiled at him. "He likes you, Daddy."

"I like him too. I'm glad he came to live with us."

"He doesn't like Devin much," Penny said.

"Oh? Why not?"

"Devin was teasing him this morning. He said Zombunny was ugly."

"What does your brother know? He's a teenager, and being obnoxious is the way they are. I'll talk to Devin and make him behave."

"Thanks, Daddy."

***

Two days later, Penny rushed in after school, crying. Sara met her in the living room. Penny's purple dress dripped, splotches of mud sprayed across it. She dragged Zombunny along the floor by one hand; he looked as ragged as she did.

"What happened?!"

Penny looked up between sobs. "Tony threw Zombunny in the mud!"

"Why?"

"We went down the hill by the creek, and Tony started teasing me about Zombunny—he and the other boys. He took Zombunny and tossed him."

"And you went in after him?"

"No," Penny said. "I shoved Tony. He went into the creek too. Then I jumped in, and Zombunny and I beat him up."

Sara did a double-take. "You *what*?"

"Well, it wasn't *me*," Penny clarified. "I grabbed Zombunny and started hitting Tony with him. Momma, will he wash? Will Zombunny be okay?"

"Are *you* okay?"

"What?" Penny looked down at herself. "Oh. I'm fine. Just dirty. I might need a bath."

"Alright, take off your shoes and leave Zombunny there on the floor. We'll go upstairs and hose you down."

"What about Zombunny?"

"He should come clean in the wash." Sara picked him up but couldn't find a laundry tag. Her eyes lingered on a dark stain on the bunny's face. She prodded it with a finger. "Penny, you didn't get poked or cut, did you?"

"I'm fine, Momma."

"This looks like blood."

"I hope it's Tony's."

"Hey—that's not nice."

"Momma, he threw Zombunny in the mud! He deserves it."

Sara set Zombunny back on the floor and helped Penny kick off her mud-caked shoes. "Let's get you washed up first, and then I'll clean Zombunny as best I can."

It took a good half-hour to get Penny showered, to change her into clean clothes, and to scrub her dress properly. Sara left Penny in her room, the dress in one hand, and she scooped up Zombunny in the other.

Her phone rang from her back pocket. Continuing to the laundry, she laid Penny's dress and Zombunny on top of the washing machine. Recognizing the number, she answered. "Hey, Sharon."

Tony's mom started in on the other line.

"Woah, hold on..." Sara sighed. "Penny said Tony took her bunny and tossed him in the creek, so she shoved him in." Sara paused as Sharon continued. "What? No, I seriously doubt Penny *bit* him. She didn't have any blood on her." Then she remembered the bunny. She turned Zombunny over again: same bright green face, now smeared in mud, but no signs of the dark stain. His long, stitched mouth looked the same. "I'll ask her, but she only said she pushed him in the creek and then clobbered him with Zombunny—her stuffed rabbit."

The call continued for a few more exchanges, but Sara ended it by telling Sharon she'd call her back. She headed upstairs. "Penny?"

Penny sat coloring on a piece of paper in her room. "Yes, Momma?"

"I just got off the phone with Tony's mom. She said he got bit."

Penny glanced up, a look on her face that seemed to say, *so what?*

"Did you bite him during your fight?"

Penny shook her head. "No. All I did was push him, and then I whacked him with Zombunny."

"She said he has a bite mark on his shoulder, and it broke the skin."

"Momma, I didn't bite him. It must have been one of the other kids."

"Was anyone else fighting with Tony?"

"Arin and Zander laughed at me. Macy was there, but she didn't do anything to Tony."

"Then who bit him?" Sara asked.

"Momma, it wasn't me. Honest."

"Okay, but who else could have bitten Tony?"

"I don't know," Penny said. A smile slowly crept onto her face. "Maybe Zombunny did it."

"Young lady, we both know stuffed animals don't bite people. I want the truth. Now. Did you bite Tony while you were fighting?"

The smile died. "No, Momma."

"Well, someone did, and if it was you, you'd better tell me, or you're going to be in trouble."

Penny stared blankly, but she said nothing.

Sara glowered. "You stay in your room until dinner."

***

Frank and Sara confronted her again after dinner, but Penny stuck to her story. She even got mad. The argument ended with Penny being punished with no movie before bed and a promise of apologizing to Tony.

The following evening, Frank secured Penny in the back seat. Zombunny, clean and tidy again, sat next to her. They occasionally talked with the Gladstones at school functions and had even gotten together with the family for dinner a couple of times. But even though they were in the same grade and class, Penny and Tony never liked playing together.

Penny sat, arms crossed, and scowled dramatically

enough to earn an award. She'd even drawn grumpy eyebrows on Zombunny's face to let Frank and Sara know her feelings about apologizing. Frank didn't show it, but he thought the eyebrows were pretty clever for a six-year-old and he ignored the quiet insurrection.

They drove to Tony's house, but Frank slowed, frowning as he approached. An ambulance sat in the driveway with two police cars on either side. Frank parked a good length back. "Hon, you okay by yourself if I check on this?" he asked. "Just for a minute."

"What's going on, Daddy?"

"I don't know. You be okay?"

"Yeah. I'll be alright."

"I won't leave sight of the car. I just want to see if I can find out what's up."

Frank shut the engine off and got out, locking Penny inside. He cut across the street and headed toward a policeman standing at the back of an ambulance. "Hi," he said. "I'm friends with the Gladstones. Is everything okay?"

"We're still getting details. You need to stay back, sir."

"Sorry. My daughter and I just came over to for a quick visit..."

The front door opened and two paramedics guided a gurney toward the back of the ambulance. Frank backed off, but not before he saw Tony on the gurney, eyes closed and wearing a respiration mask. Tony's Mom shadowed them, her eyes catching Frank's.

"What is it?" he asked.

Sharon shook her head. "He's got some infection. It's the bite Penny gave him. You should get Penny checked out, too."

"Bad?" he asked, feeling stupid as soon as the word fell out of his mouth.

"He started running a big fever last night: a hundred and four. He got delirious when Ted tried to take his temperature and bit him." Dazed and stricken, she hurried into the back end of the ambulance.

Frank returned to the car. Getting in, he turned to Penny in the back seat. The overhead light spread over her and Zombunny. Penny had erased the eyebrows on his head and written the word *Hapy*.

"What's happening, Daddy?"

"Tony's sick. How are you feeling?"

"I'm fine. Has he got the bad flu?"

"I don't know. We might have to take you to the doctor to get you checked out since you bit him."

Penny frowned. "I didn't bite him! I told you."

"Penny? Enough. We know Tony's friends didn't bite him, and you said Macy didn't. That leaves you. You need to start telling the truth, or you're going to get another punishment."

The scowl returned.

Frank drove them home and sent Penny to her room. She dragged Zombunny along with her by his small hand. Once she disappeared upstairs, Frank turned to his wife. "Tony's got some kind of infection or flu. They're taking him to the hospital."

"Oh my," Sara said. It didn't take her long to play the facts out. "Oh. If she bit Tony, we need to take her to the doctor. She's been exposed."

"So have we," Frank said. "If it's Covid, it means all of us need to be checked out."

"Crap. I'll call the hospital's main line. Dr. Zeurcher's office will be closed until the morning."

"Alright."

They ended up driving in and spent the next three hours at the hospital. They didn't get home until after Penny's bedtime. Devin added a scowl of his own, getting out of the car. "My sister the vampire."

"It's not my fault," Penny said.

"Quit biting people, and it won't be." He headed inside.

"Momma."

"Time for bed."

"I'm not a vampire," she insisted.

"No, but I hope you've learned your lesson."

Grumping and grousing, Penny stomped to her room.

***

A knock on the door the next morning roused Frank. Sara rolled over, sighing. "What now?"

"God only knows. Maybe it's good news."

Frank hopped out of bed and headed downstairs in sleep shorts and a t-shirt. He opened the door to a man and a woman in white shirts and blue jackets. They wore face masks, face shields, and gloves.

"Morning," Frank said. "Can I help you?"

The man's dark eyebrows scrunched in earnest. "We're from the CDC." They both produced identification badges. Frank looked them over and when he seemed satisfied, the man asked, "You're Mr. Frank Allen? Can we talk to you?"

"Is this about the Covid tests we had last night?"

The two traded a look. "No. This is about a boy named Tony Gladstone. We got your name from his mother, Sharon."

"We happened by their house last night. I saw them taking Tony out. Is he okay?"

"We need to know about the contact your daughter had

with him," the dark-haired woman said. "According to Tony's mother, your daughter bit him two days ago."

"Yeah. They got into a fight. Wait... We got tested last night in case we've been exposed."

"She did bite Tony Gladstone, then?"

"Yeah. Why?"

"Where did you go to get tested?" the man asked.

"The hospital. Mercy County. Why?"

"Do you remember the name of the doctor you saw?"

"No, but we've got a receipt."

"Okay, we need you to quarantine, starting now. I'll send someone up for the receipt. You don't go to the store, for walks...nothing. We need your complete cooperation."

Sara plodded down the stairs half-asleep, her bathrobe swishing along the floor.

"I guess we tested positive," Frank told her.

"No," the woman said. "We need your daughter to come in for further testing."

"If she has Covid, she can quarantine with us."

"Mr. and Mrs. Allen, Tony died this morning."

Sara gasped. Frank's eyes widened and his mind whirred. "Oh my God. From a bite? And so fast? You think Penny's infected, too? Is it Covid?"

"No," the woman said. "It's something else."

"If it wasn't Covid, then how did Tony die?" Sara asked.

"His fever rose too high, and the doctors couldn't get it down. He also turned violent. Has your daughter displayed any violent outbursts lately? Has she tried to bite anyone else?"

"No. She was grumpy at Tony... Do you know what killed him? Can you treat Penny?"

"We don't know, which is why we need all of you to come in. We've gotten ahold of the other families whose children were playing with Penny that day, but we need the names of anyone you've been in contact with since the bite."

"Wait," Frank said. "Sharon said Tony bit his dad. Is he okay?"

"He's in intensive care and exhibiting similar behaviors. We need you to pack bags and inform work you won't be coming in for several days. We're sending a van to take you."

"What's going on?" Sara asked.

"Can we count on your cooperation?"

Frank nodded. "Sure. Whatever you need."

"Thank you. We'd like to take your daughter. One of you can come with her."

Another look. "I can go," Frank said. "You get Devin and pack our things. I'll get dressed and wake Penny."

He hurried upstairs, threw on clothes, and headed for

Penny's room. She lay awake, staring at the ceiling.

"Hey hon," he said.

"What is it, Daddy?"

"I need you to put on some clothes. We need to have more tests."

"Why?"

"Because the doctors are afraid we have the big flu."

"Okay, but I'm bringing Zombunny."

"That's fine."

He helped her dress. Devin ambled by, half-asleep. "What's up, Dad?"

"We have to take Penny in for more tests. We're all being quarantined."

"Oh man. We've got it, don't we?"

"Mom will tell you what's up. Come on, Penny."

Penny snagged Zombunny by the ear on the way out the door. They grabbed jackets, Frank kissed Peg, and they headed down the steps with the CDC agents. They got in a van, Frank helping Penny with her seatbelt before climbing in next to her. The woman looked her over as the car started down the road. "Is he your friend?" she asked of the rabbit.

"Yes." Penny nodded. "This is Zombunny. He goes with me everywhere."

The blue van turned away from the hospital as they

reached the street corner. Realizing they were headed in the wrong direction, Frank perked up. "Where are we going?"

"We've got an emergency quarantine site set up."

"Exactly how many people are getting these life-threatening symptoms?"

"Only Tony, his dad, and the two doctors who restrained Tony."

"Just what's happening to them?" Frank asked.

"The same symptoms. High fever followed by extreme violent outbursts."

"And you think this started because of my daughter?"

"We don't know. We've traced the Gladstone family's interactions and no one else has displayed symptoms. It started with him. Are you sure your daughter hasn't had a fever?"

"No," Frank said, feeling Penny's forehead—cool to the touch. Zombunny sat on the seat next to her, sporting eyebrows again. His face held a menacing quality now. "You do like drawing eyebrows, don't you?"

She glanced over at Zombunny. "He's happy Tony died."

"Penny Rose Allen!" Frank said, leveling the Dad Face at her. "Wait...how did you know Tony died?"

"Zombunny told me."

"When?"

"This morning, before you came to get me."

Frank took a long look at her. She seemed okay, but what came out of her mouth wasn't normal. They'd talked about Tony having violent outbursts. He stared at Penny's face, looking for some sign of anger, but she only gazed out the window.

"She must have heard us from the door," Frank told the CDC woman, who watched them in the rear-view mirror.

They drove out past the highway along a lonely county road. Several minutes ticked by before Frank spotted a series of abandoned warehouses set at the edge of a cornfield.

"Just what kind of tests are you going to perform?" he asked.

"Mostly blood draws at this point, but they'll be testing for all kinds of things, including rabies."

"Rabies? I thought you had to be bitten by a rodent or a raccoon to get rabies."

"Has your daughter been bitten by anything recently?"

Frank thought back over the last few weeks. He started shaking his head before he answered. "Nothing I can think of. I'd remember if she'd gotten an animal bite."

Inside, they were led through a series of corridors before being deposited in what looked like an average doctor's suite. Frank helped Penny on to the end of an examination bed. A nurse entered in a blue hazmat suit. She carried a tray. "Hey there, sweetie," she said through her hood. "I'm Nurse Avery, and I'm going to take some blood."

"I don't like needles," Penny said.

"I can imagine. Well, I'm really good at making it quick and not hurting. I've been doing this a long time. Think you can trust me?"

"It won't hurt?"

"It will feel like a pinch, but you can hold on tight to your friend there. What is he?"

Penny brightened, holding Zombunny up. "He's new. I got him, and he's the softest bunny in the whole world."

The nurse ran a gloved hand over his forehead. "He is really soft. You hold him tight with one arm, and I'll get what I need really quick. Does that sound okay?"

Penny thought it over. "Yeah," she finally said.

Frank patted her shoulder. "I'll be here with you, hon. It's like the nurse said—be over fast."

"Okay."

Nurse Avery went to work and prepared her arm. "Look at your father. People tell me it hurts even less when you don't look."

Penny turned toward Frank, her arm snaked around Zombunny's neck. But when the nurse poked her arm,

Penny's eyes widened. "Ow!"

Before Nurse Avery could apologize, Penny shifted her grip on Zombunny and smacked the nurse on the shoulder. Nurse Avery cried out, dropping the needle. She backed away and grabbed her shoulder. Frank's eyes widened. Blood ran down the woman's arm, a hole torn in her blue suit. Nurse Avery gave them a horrified look and backed out the door.

Frank's eyes narrowed as he turned toward Penny. She balanced Zombunny on her lap and rubbed at the inside of her elbow, blood smeared on her fingers. Frank grabbed a Kleenex box from a table and yanked out several. "Hang on, hon," he said and pressed the wad of tissue against the bloody spot on her arm. "It'll be okay. We'll just hold this on the spot until I can get you a band-aid."

"She told me it would only pinch!" Penny growled. Her face scrunched up into a snarl.

Frank glanced down. A large dark stain splotched across Zombunny's stitched mouth. He only frowned and pushed Penny's hand over the tissue. "Hold that in place a sec. Can I see Zombunny?"

"Okay, Daddy. He didn't mean to hurt her, but she lied about it not hurting."

Frank picked up the bunny, staring at its face. The eyebrows were back, but they were thick like rainbows, giving its face a peaceful look. Tentatively, he reached out with a finger toward the stain across its mouth.

He pushed inward.

Softness. Nothing hard, nothing sharp. He pressed back into Zombunny's head with more fingers, but felt nothing which could have torn through the nurse's hazmat suit, let alone able to cut her arm.

"Penny?"

"Yes, Daddy?"

"Did Zombunny bite the nurse?"

"Yeah," she said.

"Because she hurt you? Like Tony did?"

"Yes, Daddy. Zombunny said he'll always protect me."

Frank looked at his daughter. "Is the nurse going to get sick like Tony did?"

Penny stared down at her Kleenex. "I don't know. I don't know why Tony got sick."

Two people in hazmat suits entered the room. Frank remembered one as the CDC agent who'd come to the house.

"She bit Nurse Avery?" the man asked.

Frank shook his head. "No. Penny was sitting on the bed. She hit the nurse with the bunny." He held Zombunny by the back of its neck and lifted it up. "See the blood stain?"

The agent backed off a step. "Is there something sharp inside it?"

"I didn't feel anything." He held up a finger but realized he had blood on the tip. He cursed and set the bunny on the counter next to a sink. Immediately, he started scrubbing the blood off.

"Mr. Allen, can we take a look at the doll?"

"What? Sure." He finished scouring his hands with soap. Drying with handfuls of paper towels from a dispenser, he spied sanitizer and squeezed a massive pile into his palms. "I don't have any cuts on my hands. I should be safe, right?"

The second man inspected his finger. "You don't have any broken skin. You should be fine."

The agent picked up Zombunny and pressed a finger around the backside of its head. After prodding at different areas, he sighed. "Doctor Parsons, I can't find any hard edges or sharp points." He turned to Penny. "Did you bite the nurse?"

"No," she replied sternly. "She stabbed me with her needle, and it hurt. Zombunny got her."

The agent studied her and her dress. "We're going to borrow your bunny for a bit. Okay?"

"You'll clean the blood off his mouth?"

The agent seized on the idea. "Yes, we'll clean him up for

you."

Penny thought it over. "Okay. Just don't hurt him."

"We won't, sweetie. I'll bring him back in a few minutes."

Heading for the door, the agent carried Zombunny gingerly. Frank's eyes widened. He spotted the word *back* in dark letters on Zombunny's forehead and the word *soon* on his belly above the skull and crossbones.

Frank got out his phone, pulled up a number, and waited through the rings while glancing at the clock on the wall. He couldn't remember what time they opened. It rang four times, and someone picked up.

"Dancing Spider, this is Kacey."

"Uh, hi. My name is Frank Allen. I was in a couple of weeks ago with my daughter, and we bought a green plush bunny. It was kind of creepy looking."

A pause played out. "Oh, yeah. I remember. I checked you out. What can I do for you?"

"Do you know where you got it from?" Frank laughed. "It probably sounds funny, but we were trying to... Well, we were thinking about getting one for one of my sister's kids, and I wanted to know if you had more or knew where you got them."

"Yeah, it was a weird thing. Hang on. Cheryl's in the back—I can ask her."

He waited, glancing at Penny. "What'cha doing, Daddy?"

"Oh. I just want to talk to the nice lady who sold us Zombunny."

"How come?"

"I was just curious to see if she knew how to get blood off of him."

"Silly. Just wash him with soap and water like Mommy did."

Someone picked up the phone. "Hello?" said a different voice.

"Uh, yeah. I was just talking to the other woman," Frank said. "We bought the zombie bunny from your store, and I was wondering if you could tell me where you got it from?"

"I bought a bunch of international toys about a month back. We got things from all kinds of places overseas. I got a shipment from Panama and some other Central American countries. I didn't remember seeing the rabbit, but Kacey said he was bright green. It's funny—I should have remembered it, but it might have gotten crammed in a pile of other things."

"Was he the only one?"

"Yeah. We didn't get a lot of stuffed animals. There're customs issue with plush toys sometimes."

"This might sound odd, but you two haven't been bitten recently, have you?"

"Bitten? By an animal? Or by a bug?"

"I don't know. I hadn't thought of a bug or a spider."

"Did your daughter get bit?"

"No," Frank said. He weighed saying anything, knowing the CDC would be heading to them next. "Penny—my daughter, she hit some kid with her bunny, and he got bit by something. Maybe on or in the bunny. But, it—he's not doing well."

"Oh my gosh! Is your daughter okay?"

"Yes. Uhm, we're being checked out. Someone may come to visit you in connection with it."

"Crap. Okay. Can I do anything for you from here?"

"No. I don't know exactly what's going on, but I'm guessing I'll know more soon."

"I'm writing your name down. Frank, you said?"

"Yes, Frank Allen."

"Okay. I've got your number from this call. Please call me back when you get more information. I'm sorry for her friend."

"I'll call. Thanks." He hung up.

The door opened, and the male agent reentered. "Mr. Allen, how long has your daughter had her stuffed rabbit?"

Frank started nodding. "A few weeks. I just got off

the phone with the store owner. It's called the Dancing Spider—downtown in a mall. They carry all kinds of eclectic toys. She said they got a shipment from Panama."

"Okay. We'll send people over there. Your wife and son are here. We're going to keep you together."

"How's the nurse?"

"We flushed the wound, and we'll isolate her." He turned to Penny. "We're going to run some tests on your bunny. Okay?"

"Just don't hurt him," Penny said. "He won't like it."

The agent cast a nervous look from behind the faceplate in his hood. The door opened, and Sara and Devin slipped in.

"I'll let you get settled," the agent said. "The phone is on the counter. Dial zero, and someone will help you. If you need bathrooms or food or anything else, just ask. I'm afraid we're going to keep you overnight. We've got TVs and a game system if the kids are interested."

"Okay," Frank said. "We'll get settled in."

"I'm sorry for all of this, but we're not sure what we're dealing with." The agent left.

"Frank, what's going on?" Sara asked.

"It bit one of the nurses."

Sara's eyes narrowed. "What bit one of the nurses?"

"Penny's rabbit."

Sara shot him a look. "Are you messing with me?"

Frank threw his hands in the air. "A nurse came in to take blood. Penny cried out when she got stuck, and she hit the nurse with Zombunny. I didn't exactly see it, but where Penny whacked her, it tore her suit, and she got bit on the shoulder."

"Serious?" Devin asked.

"I don't know. Penny was sitting. She was nowhere near the woman's shoulder."

"Penny?" Sara asked. "Is what Daddy said true?"

She looked up blankly. "Yes. Zombunny bit the nurse. She poked me with the needle, and he got mad."

"How...how do you know he got mad?"

"He doesn't like people hurting me. It's why he bit Tony. He thought about biting Devin for picking on him, but I told Zombunny it's just the way most teenagers act. Like Daddy said."

"You talk to him?" Frank asked.

"We talk all the time. Can't you hear him, Daddy? He writes messages on his forehead for me, too."

A commotion erupted outside their room. Shouts came from multiple directions. Their door had a frosted half window, through which the Frank saw several people hurry past. He could swear some of the silhouettes belonged to armed soldiers. Sara backed away, one hand pulling Devin with her. She huddled next to Penny and Frank. "I don't like this."

People called out. There came the unmistakable sound of a gunshot.

"*Frank*," Sara muttered.

"Let's stay here." He checked their door. It didn't lock from the inside. The half window showed more people rushing past. He hesitated, looking around for something to jam against the door, but there was nothing but the bed.

More gunshots. Screams echoed somewhere in the facility.

"Mommy!" Penny shouted. "What's happening? Where's Zombunny?"

Sara slipped an arm around her. "I'm not sure, honey, but we'll be alright. We're going to stay right here until things calm down."

"Those were gunshots," Devin said.

Frank shook his head, gesturing toward Penny with his eyes.

An automatic rifle rattled through the air and then abruptly stopped. They heard people running; screaming drowned out everything else, and then...

Footsteps.

A slow, steady clack of shoes on the tile flooring. One after the other, they grew louder with each click. Frank stuffed his foot against the base of the door and held the knob with both hands. A shadow stopped in front of their small window. Sara sucked in a breath. Frank leaned away from the frosted glass as best he could, his fingers locked tight around the handle.

Silence stretched out, seconds dragging.

The shadow dropped, and something thumped against the floor. Frank listened, eager for some sound, but everything had stilled. No more footsteps, no cries, no gunfire...nothing.

A soft knocking started on the door. It started as four raps. Frank looked back. Sara shook her head fiercely. Devin clenched her around the waist. Only Penny looked unflustered.

"Go ahead, Daddy. You can open the door."

"Who is it?" he asked.

"It's okay."

Tap, tap, tap.

He bit his lip and carefully turned the handle. Edging his foot back an inch, he slowly opened the door a couple of inches. On the floor lay a man in a blue hazmat suit, a hole torn at the back of his neck. Next to the door, Zombunny sat propped against the frame.

Penny jumped off the end of the bed and darted forward. Sara yelled for her to stop, but she reached Frank.

"Open it, Daddy. It's alright."

He opened the door further. More bodies were strewn about the floor further down the hall. One of them started twitching. Penny slipped a hand out through the opening and pulled Zombunny inside. A long smear of blood ran across the length of his face. Frank watched as the blood drained into the plush material. The dark stain receded.

He closed the door and backed up. "What is your bunny doing?"

"He's creating more friends, Daddy. He told me he's going to clean humanity."

The blood completely dissipated from Zombunny's face, his fur clean and dry.

"Hon," Sara said. "What are you talking about? He's just a stuffed animal."

"Oh no, Mommy," Penny said. "He's real. He told me his secret name—he said I could tell you."

"What's his real name?" Frank asked.

She grinned. "He's got a big long name—I can't say it, but he said it's okay to call him Tez Cat."

Frank shook his head.

"It's okay, Daddy. He said he'll protect us from his other friends. He likes us. We just have to stay here for a while, and then we can go home."

"Why?" he asked. "What's going to happen?"

"He said there are too many bad people in the world, so he's going to make lots of friends and make it good again. We just have to stay here. Don't worry, Daddy. He'll protect us."

Penny held Zombunny up for them to see. The word *new* appeared on his forehead. On his belly, just above the black skull and crossbones, two more words appeared in the green material: *wrld soon*.

Craig Crawford grew up reading, but upon discovering fantasy and science fiction, he wondered if he could do it too. In 2019, he added horror to his genres and got his first story published. Since, he's published twenty-eight short stories, including a humorous novella. Last year he published a novel length dark sci-fi/horror serial thanks to RedCape Publishing, and he's currently working on the next installment. He writes in horror, fantasy, sci-fi, YA, humor—whatever his imagination gives him.

You can learn more about him at
craiglcrawfordbooks.com

You can find out more about his serial at
projectthreshold.com

CONTENT WARNINGS

Please note: because this is horror, it should be assumed that
the basic horror tropes will apply.
These include death, gore, and violence.

death of a child